T☢XIC

" 'It's bizarre, isn't it?' Nico said to Ella. 'We know how to use knives and forks, we know how to load a dishwasher, but we know nothing about our lives before today.

'It's like we've all been programmed.' **"**

ROBOTS
V HUMANS

Robots v Humans
by Jonny Zucker
Illustrated by Alan Brown

Published by Ransom Publishing Ltd.
Radley House, 8 St. Cross Road, Winchester, Hampshire
SO23 9HX, UK
www.ransom.co.uk

ISBN   978 178127 717 1
First published in 2015

ROBOTS
V HUMANS

JONNY ZUCKER

ILLUSTRATED BY
ALAN BROWN

Ransom

Chapter 1

The metal door slammed shut and Nico found himself in a large high-ceilinged room.

He looked to his right and saw five kids his age: two boys and three girls.

They looked as confused as he felt.

A door at the far end of the room swung open and a tall, slim man with a bald head and sunglasses strode forwards.

When he was a few feet away he stopped and took off his shades. His eyes were a striking emerald green.

'Welcome!' he said, smiling and looking at each one of them in turn. 'I'm delighted you all made it safely.'

Nico and the others frowned, because none of them had any idea where they were or how they'd got there.

'My name is Jensen Hazard,' said the man, 'and I will be your host for the next few days. I am here to look after you and to attend to all of your needs. This is my project and you are here as my guests.

'I will begin by explaining a little bit about you.'

Nico narrowed his eyes. He tried to remember how he'd got here. Had he walked? Caught a bus? He couldn't remember.

Nor could he remember where he lived, or whether he had any brothers or sisters, or what his favourite music was, or anything else …

His thoughts were interrupted by Hazard.

'Three of you were frozen at birth and woken up today, on your fifteenth birthday,' explained Hazard.

'You three are in excellent health. In fact you are just like any other human, but you will have absolutely no recall of anything that happened before you walked into this room just now.'

'What about the other three?' asked Nico, his voice sounding strange and unfamiliar, his brain trying to take in what Hazard had just said.

'The other three of you are robots,' replied Hazard. 'You have been made to the most incredibly high standard and, as such, it is impossible to tell you apart from real human beings.'

'Which of us is which?' asked one of the girls, who had bleached-blonde hair and large, royal-blue eyes.

'Ah ha,' beamed Hazard, 'that is where the fun comes in. I will not be telling you – at least, not yet.

'You will be living here together this week and carrying out a series of tasks and activities. Some of these tasks will set you against each other; some will see you working as a team.

'I will be studying your actions and behaviour very closely, and this will give me a chance to analyse how well the humans perform and how well the robots perform.'

'So *you* know which of us is which?' asked a boy with thick eyebrows and a dimple in his chin.

'Absolutely,' nodded Hazard. 'And when the time is right I will pass this information on to you. But, for the time being, you don't need to worry about that. And, as I'm sure you are hungry, I suggest you all go and eat.'

A blue panel at the side of the room slid open. Delicious cooking smells wafted out.

'Eat and enjoy!' said Hazard, walking in the opposite direction. 'I will see you in a short while.'

Nico stepped into the dining room with the others, his brain filled with burning questions.

Was he human? Or was he a robot?

He *felt* human, or at least he thought he did, but then Hazard had said that you couldn't tell robots and humans apart.

Nico couldn't remember anything before today. Did that mean he was a human, just woken up? Or was he a robot who'd been created in the last few days?

With these questions threatening to overpower him, Nico decided to block them out for a while and grab something to eat. He'd return to them when his belly was full.

CHAPTER 2

The dining room was rectangular in shape, with pale yellow wallpaper and a sink, fridge, dishwasher and cooker at the far end. A large wooden table with benches on either side stood in the centre.

Sparkling white china bowls containing bread, cheeses, rice, fresh vegetables, noodles and fruit were set out on the table.

The six all sat down to eat, but before they began to tuck in they exchanged names.

The bleached-blonde girl was called Ella. The bushy eyebrows guy was Tom. A girl with a thin face and a tightly scraped back ponytail was named Jessica; a boy with a sharp nose and red cheeks was Jules, and a girl with high cheekbones and a ready smile was called Keisha.

'This is so weird,' said Ella, taking a plate and putting various foodstuffs on it. 'That Hazard guy is right. I can't remember anything before just now.'

'Me neither,' said Jules. 'But which of us are robots and which of us are humans? If he's not going to tell us, should we try to find out ourselves?'

They looked each other up and down, trying to spot any robotic signs, but none were there.

'I wouldn't mind being a robot,' smiled Nico, helping himself to some rice. 'If I were, I might have special powers.'

'I think I'm probably one of the robots,' said Tom, trapping a piece of lettuce on his fork. 'No disrespect to any of you, but it looks like I'm the tallest and strongest.'

'Don't bet on that,' hit back Ella. 'Looks aren't everything.'

They spent the rest of the meal talking about their lack of personal history and what sort of tasks Hazard might have in store for them.

*****

When they'd finished eating, they placed their plates and cutlery in the dishwasher and Nico switched it on.

'It's bizarre, isn't it?' he said to Ella. 'We know how to use knives and forks, we know how to load a dishwasher, but we know nothing about our lives before today. It's like we've all been programmed.'

'Well, if Hazard is telling the truth,' replied Ella, 'the only past the humans here have is being cooped up in some icy chamber after their parents gave them away – if that's what happened. And the robots presumably came from a kit, so their only relation is a cardboard box.'

Nico laughed.

'Or he's lying,' butted in Keisha, 'and we're all robots, made by him and controlled by him.'

Nico frowned. That didn't sound good.

At that moment a red door next to a stack of shelves opened and they heard Hazard calling them through.

Inside was a high-tech gym with six sets of shiny silver and black equipment. These included a rowing machine, an exercise bike and a running treadmill.

Hazard was sitting at a desk on the far side of the room, studying a computer screen.

'OK,' he announced, looking up. 'I want everyone to wear one of these on their T shirts. This piece of kit will monitor your heart rate, your body mass index and lots of other data.'

He stood up and handed a white disc to everyone. Nico stuck his onto his shirt.

'Right,' said Hazard. 'I want you all to choose a machine. You will have ten minutes to perform to the peak of your strength on this machine. We will then have a two-minute break and you will move in a clockwise direction onto the next piece of equipment.

'We will do this until you've all been at every station. Everyone understand?'

They nodded.

'Excellent,' said Hazard, setting his stopwatch. 'Please begin ... NOW!'

Chapter 3

Nico went for the running machine. It started up the second he stepped onto it. He was aware of the others choosing various pieces of equipment, but he focused on the task in hand.

In thirty seconds he'd developed a good running rhythm and was pleased to discover he had plenty of energy and strong legs.

After exactly ten minutes all of the machines automatically slowed down and then stopped. Everyone got a breather and a drink, while Hazard tapped away on his computer.

Next up, Nico moved to the rowing machine. Again he worked hard at it without feeling too much strain. Following that he was on a steps machine.

An hour and fifteen minutes later, everyone had done everything.

'Excellent,' nodded Hazard, collecting back the chest monitors and closing down his computer. 'You are all in excellent physical shape. Now, for a bit of fun, which of you can catch these?'

He pulled three very small purple balls out of his pocket and threw them into the air. Immediately they started flying around

the room at incredible speed, bouncing off the walls, ceiling and floor.

'Well, go on then,' laughed Hazard. 'Try and get them.'

Instantly all six of them were racing round the room, jumping and leaping and trying to catch the tiny purple balls.

Jessica caught the first after jumping off a chair and grabbing it. Tom nabbed the second and Nico, after launching himself off the bar on the running machine, trapped the third.

'My catch was easily the best,' boasted Tom, as they handed the balls back to Hazard.

'It *so* wasn't,' hit back Ella. 'Nico's was far better.'

Tom scowled at her.

'Gather round please,' said Hazard.

When they were standing in a group, Hazard put the balls away and turned to face them.

'You've done well so far,' he nodded, 'so congratulations. As I said, my whole aim here is to see if young human people and robots can get along together. Over the next few days we'll put this to further tests.'

'Where are we going to sleep?' asked Jessica.

'I could do with a shower,' said Jules.

'I will come to all of that in a moment,' said Hazard, 'but first I want to tell you something.'

They all leaned in a bit.

'I want you to know that you are all here voluntarily. Any of you can leave at any time.

'But I should warn you. The parents of the humans among you agreed to give you up at birth for a very large sum of money. They signed a contract stating that they would never attempt to see you again and that they would ensure you would never find out who they were.

'So the humans amongst you have no family and no home to go to.'

Nico raised an eyebrow. The others looked equally startled.

'The robots obviously have no families,' went on Hazard, 'but none of you are to worry about this. When you are done here, I

27

have selected six families who will take each of you in as if you are one of their own. No money has been exchanged over this; they all want you.

'Needless to say, they will not know that some of you are robots: they will naturally think that you are all human.

'When we are finished, I will reveal the identity of these families and you will go to live with them.'

'Could that ever change?' asked Ella. 'You know, the bit about real parents never seeing their child again?

'No,' replied Hazard, with a look of steely determination suddenly appearing on his face.

'That is set in stone. You will NEVER, EVER meet your real parents.'

CHAPTER 4

The teenagers slept in two dorms – one for the boys and one for the girls.

Out of the dorm windows Nico saw a high barbed-wire fence surrounding the place. The building they were in seemed to be some kind of old country house.

The fence made him think that, in spite of what Hazard had said, leaving here whenever you wanted to was probably not an option.

Nico had a shower and climbed into his bed; he'd chosen the one next to the window.

'I'm first on the leader board so far,' crowed Tom, lying on his bed with his hands behind his head.

'That's rubbish,' said Jules, 'and anyway who cares? It's not like there's going to be a prize or anything; Hazard would have said something if there was.'

'I wouldn't be so sure about that,' said Tom, as he turned over to go to sleep.

*****

The next morning, after breakfast in the dining room, Hazard appeared. He asked if they'd slept well and then led them outside.

At the back of the building was a big area of grass and at the far side were three metal figures, painted in khaki and standing about six feet tall.

'This,' said Hazard, 'is a team activity. When we are ready to start, those figures will produce guns. They are not real guns; they fire plastic non-lethal pellets. However, these pellets do sting on impact. For that reason you will all wear goggles during this activity.'

He handed out six sets of goggles and everyone put them on.

'As soon as the figures start firing, your job is to reach them and disarm them in the quickest time possible. They are sensitive to movement and will be constantly tracking all of you.'

Nico's body tensed. This didn't look easy.

He was right.

As soon as Hazard pressed a switch on his mobile phone, metal guns appeared at the figures' sides and the pellets started flying.

At first the six of them ran all over the grass like crazy, trying to avoid the pellets, but it wasn't long before Nico and Ella marshalled the troops together and got them working in pairs, with one as the decoy and the other as the attacker.

Nico teamed up with Ella and he took the role of decoy. The figure on the right traced Nico's movements and unleashed volleys of pellets at him, while Ella crawled through the grass making herself as low as possible.

Nico took a series of hits, in the chest, on the arm and on his legs. Each one stung badly, but he was determined to help take his enemy down.

In the end it was he and Ella together who reached the figure and with lightning-quick movements dragged its gun away. They were the first pair to do so, but were followed pretty quickly by Jules and Jessica, then Tom and Keisha.

Tom was moaning about how Nico and Ella had an unfair advantage because their figure didn't fire as many shots as his one did, but the others ignored him.

There was no sign of Hazard, so they started walking back towards the building.

They hadn't got far when a fourth metal figure suddenly sprung up on the grass behind them and fired a powerful shot that hit Ella on the back.

She cried out in pain and crashed to the ground.

Chapter 5

As Keisha ran to Ella's side, Nico raced towards the fourth figure, dodging pellets and shouting in fury.

He launched himself into the air and high-kicked the gun out of his attacker's hands. He then ran back to the others.

For a few seconds he thought Ella was dead, as her body was totally motionless, but in fact she'd just blacked out. Five seconds later, when she opened her eyes, he breathed a deep sigh of relief.

'Ow,' she said, feeling her back.

Nico was helping her to her feet when Hazard came striding over.

'That wasn't fair!' snapped Nico. 'You never said anything about a fourth figure.'

'Of course I didn't,' replied Hazard sternly. 'It comes under the category of unexpected events. I thought you dealt with it rather well.'

'Well this whole activity wasn't fair,' whined Tom. 'The figures fired at different rates.'

'Life is rarely fair,' said Hazard, his eyes boring into Tom's.

Tom said nothing and walked away.

*****

The rest of the morning and most of the afternoon (after a healthy lunch) were spent in a comfortable lounge with plush armchairs and sofas.

Hundreds of wooden and metal puzzles had been set out on low tables and the participants had to solve as many as possible within strict time limits. As they twisted, pulled and turned these objects, Hazard walked around the room making notes on a clipboard.

Nico managed to solve his first six puzzles with relative ease, but the seventh was a knot of wooden blocks that you had to separate and turn into a straight line. It was extremely hard and totally frustrating.

He cracked it finally, with some help from Ella, and was pleased he could repay the favour when he helped her untangle a sprawling mesh of steel.

*****

As with all meal times, Hazard wasn't around when they ate supper. The food was good and they all ate hungrily.

'I still think my gun-toting figure fired more rapidly than the others,' moaned Tom, looking round the table for any supporters of his theory. But he didn't get any.

Ella just said, 'For one second, Tom, can you stop being so competitive?'

That shut him up.

After supper, they went into the lounge.
All of the puzzles had been tidied away and
a pile of books and magazines had been left
on the table.

Nico flopped down onto a sofa with a
sports book and started reading the first
chapter. Bits of it seemed vaguely familiar,
but whether this was because he was a
human or a robot with implanted
knowledge was impossible to tell.

Ella sat beside him with a thick book
about the history of martial arts. Tom sat in
an armchair sulking, while Jules and Keisha
played draughts.

Jessica announced she was going outside
to get some fresh air and asked if anyone
wanted to join her. As she got no takers, she
said she'd be back soon and calmly strolled
off.

It wasn't long before she returned though, and this time she wasn't calm. She was in a terrible state.

'There's an outbuilding on the other side of the lawn,' she panted, 'and it's on fire! I heard barking coming from inside it. I think there's a dog trapped in there!'

In an instant Nico and the others sprang to their feet, left the room and sprinted as fast as they could towards the fire.

CHAPTER 6

Out of the main building burst the six teenagers, down a path at the side and out onto the lawn.

At the far left end was a run-down, two-storey brown building. Flames were coming out of the windows on the top floor and a huge cloud of dirty smoke was floating above the structure.

As they got nearer they heard the high-pitched, panicked bark of not one, but two, dogs.

'OK,' shouted Nico, immediately taking charge. 'Tom and Jessica – go and look for fire extinguishers. Keisha and Jules – see if there's any way in round the back. Ella and I will go straight in.'

'I think I should go in,' said Tom, 'seeing as I'm probably the bravest.'

'This is not the time for point scoring!' snapped Ella. 'Just get on with it.'

Tom scowled at her and then turned and ran with Jessica back to the main house.

Nico pulled off his hoodie and wrapped it round his face so that it covered his nose and his mouth. Ella did the same with her jumper. She gave him a thumbs-up and they ran inside.

The fire hadn't yet spread to the lower level and they made it up the stairs quickly. But as soon as they reached the upper level the heat hit them like a wall from hell. Flames were climbing along the floorboards and up the doorframes.

The dogs' barking was getting louder and more distressed.

'I think they're in there,' shouted Nico, pointing to a room at the end of the corridor.

'Do you think we can make it?' yelled Ella anxiously.

'We've got to try,' cried Nico. 'Come on.'

With the sizzling heat almost engulfing them, they stepped over lines of fire and swerved round a falling piece of fiery wood.

Both of them started coughing, their makeshift masks unable to protect them from smoke this dense.

Ella kicked a burning suitcase out of their way and they ploughed on. The door at the end was closed. Nico grabbed the metal handle and screamed out in pain. It was red-hot. He wrapped his shirt cuff around his hand and quickly twisted the handle.

The door opened and they stepped in. The room was ablaze but, crouching down as low as they could get, they could see two small puppies in the corner, barking in terror.

'Look out!' screamed Nico, as a chunk of the ceiling dislodged itself. Ella dived to one

side as it came crashing onto the floor. They made it to the corner.

Nico reached forward and picked up one dog while Ella grabbed the other.

They had just started moving back across the room when there was a mini-explosion and an even bigger chunk of flaming plasterboard fell down from the ceiling and blocked the doorway.

Nico and Ella looked at each other in horror.

They were trapped.

Chapter 7

At that moment there was the loud sound of glass smashing as Keisha broke the window from outside with a large branch.

She and Tom had found a ladder round the back of the outbuilding and she was now frantically clearing shards of glass from the window edges.

'Pass it over!' she screamed.

Nico gave her the first puppy. She took it and handed it down to Jules, who was standing further down the ladder.

'There's two of them!' yelled Nico, passing her the second dog. Both dogs carried on barking frantically.

Keisha took it and shouted, 'Now, you two – get out!'

Nico beckoned for Ella to go first, but she shook her head.

There was no time to argue, so Nico climbed out and descended the ladder. Ella followed a few seconds later, but to Nico's horror the back of her shirt had caught fire.

He was about to take his own shirt off and beat the fire out when Tom and Jessica arrived with a fire extinguisher. Jessica immediately fired it at Ella's back and quickly put out the flames.

Thankfully Ella wasn't badly burnt.

A split-second later, to everyone's amazement, the fire and smoke instantly disappeared and Jensen Hazard walked round the corner.

Nico and the others turned their gaze from the now totally fire-free building to Hazard, and then back again.

'Well done all of you,' beamed Hazard. 'You passed that group task with flying colours.'

'That was a … simulation? A test?' asked Nico, in total shock.

'Totally lifelike, but yes, a simulation,' replied Hazard. 'I think you'll also find that those loveable mutts aren't as real as they look or sound.'

Everyone turned to face the dogs as Hazard tapped a button on his phone. Immediately the dogs stopped breathing and barking. They stood still like statues.

'They're robots!' said Nico, alarm showing on his face.

'But the fire was real,' said Ella. 'We felt it.'

'Of course it was real,' replied Hazard, 'but I have total control of when it comes on and when it goes off.'

'But Nico and Ella could have died in there!' protested Keisha angrily.

'I'd never have let it get that far,' said Hazard. 'It was completely safe.'

*****

That night everyone was quiet and lost in their own thoughts.

The 'fire' had spooked them and they were all angry with Hazard. Ella was still very shaken from being set on fire and Nico went over and over the terror he'd felt when the doorway had become blocked. He didn't care whether he was a robot or a human: he'd been sure he was going to die in there.

*****

The next morning Hazard let them sleep late. They woke to a relaxed breakfast.

When they'd all eaten he called them together in a narrow green passageway in front of a black door.

'I understand that yesterday's task caused you all a lot of stress,' he said, 'but it was a necessary part of your time here. I am now going to introduce you to your next activity. It will be your biggest challenge yet.'

Nico swallowed nervously.

Hazard pushed open the black door and led them inside.

CHAPTER 8

They found themselves in a huge, grey oval room.

'What is this place?' asked Keisha.

'Welcome to the Survival Lab,' said Hazard proudly, 'a place where your physical and mental abilities will be pushed to their limits.'

'Nothing can be worse than that fire,' said Ella edgily.

'What's the task?' demanded Tom.

Hazard tapped a button on his phone and, with a low whirring sound, a huge pole with a steel spike on its end shot down from an opening in the ceiling. Keisha and Jules had to move aside quickly to stop the spike from hitting them.

Hazard tapped his phone again and the spike retracted into the ceiling.

Nico looked up and saw a series of similar openings in the ceiling. Were there spiked poles behind these as well? If so, was Hazard going to really use such dangerous items in an activity?

Hazard then tapped another button and a gigantic gust of wind started blowing through the room. It was only by clutching onto each other that the teenagers managed to stay on their feet.

Hazard quickly stopped the wind.

At the tap of another button, a series of small rocks began hurtling round the room at high speed. One hit Jules on the leg and he yelped in pain. Hazard stopped the rocks and moved quickly to the door.

'OK,' he smiled. 'You have seen what you're up against. It would be hard enough to face these attacks in the light. But you are going to be doing it in the dark.'

He stepped out of the room and tapped another button on his phone. The door instantly locked and the lights went out.

'YOU CAN'T DO THIS!' yelled Ella, but it was too late. Before the six of them could talk to each other and try to work out a survival strategy, the ferocious wind swept through the room.

Nico was knocked to the floor and it was only with a forceful effort that he managed to get to his feet again.

A second later he wished he hadn't, as a volley of rocks flew towards him and one whacked him on the back of the neck. He screamed in pain and, pushing against the wind, tried to make it to where he thought one side of the room was.

He could hear the others crying out and screaming. It didn't matter if Nico was a robot or a human – one thing was sure: Hazard was a monster.

Only a monster would play this sort of game on a bunch of teenagers.

Nico stumbled forward and crashed into someone. Was it Ella or Keisha? He couldn't tell.

He struggled forwards and then heard a sinister swooping sound above him. At the last second he looked up and saw the glint of a steel spike heading straight through the darkness, towards his head.

CHAPTER 9

In terror, Nico dived to his right and rolled over, almost directly into the path of another descending spike.

He gasped in relief, but thought about the others. Had anyone been killed? He wouldn't be surprised in this room of nightmares.

Another rock hit him, this time on the ear. White-hot pain travelled down to his cheek. He was now on his hands and knees, the wind careering into him like a vicious gale. He heard someone shriek in agony and saw several spikes pumping down towards the ground.

On he crawled, reaching out and finally feeling a wall. He pressed himself against it and, using the light on his watch, spotted some kind of small box stuck to the wall.

He knew what it was; it was a fuse box.

He flipped open the lid and pressed down on as many switches as he could.

The spike poles suddenly stopped in mid-air, the wind vanished, the rocks tumbled to the floor – and the lights came on.

Nico stood up and looked around. The others were scattered around the room, sitting or lying on the floor. They all looked bruised, beaten and terrified.

Moments later the door flew open and a seething Hazard stormed in.

'What do you think you're doing?' he screamed at Nico, waving at the open fuse box. 'Who said you could interrupt this task?'

Nico struggled to his feet and stumbled towards Hazard, equally furious.

'I'll tell you what we're *not* doing,' snarled Nico. 'We're *not* doing anything else you tell us to do. We could have been burned to death in that fire or killed in this appalling place.'

'I'm totally with you, Nico!' shouted Ella, scrabbling to her feet.

The other four nodded their heads and stood up.

'OK, OK,' said Hazard, speaking more softly.

'Maybe this activity was a bit too much for you. We can forget about it and move on to something less stressful.'

'No!' snapped Nico. 'You don't understand. We're not doing anything else. You said half of us are robots and half of us are human, but you won't say who's who. You're playing with us like this is some kind of game. We don't trust you and we're not helping you any more.

'We're done here.'

There was a long pause.

'OK,' said Hazard finally, holding up his hands.

Then there was another long pause, as if Hazard was trying to decide what to do.

'I'll come clean with you,' he said at last.

'Really?' demanded Keisha.

Hazard stared at each of the teenagers in turn.

Then he spoke.

'None of you are robots. You are all human children. You were all frozen at birth. Your parents volunteered you for the programme and took the cash. That's the truth.'

The six of them looked at each other in confusion and shock.

'Why did you lie to us at the start, then?' scowled Jules.

'I thought that if I said you were all humans, you might just get up and leave. If I said some of you were robots, I figured you'd all stay to the end to find out what you were. I desperately need a batch of young humans to study for the future of my kind.'

'What do you mean?' snapped Ella.

'Oh I get it,' murmured Nico. He had spotted a tiny length of blue wire sticking out of a small panel at the back of Hazard's shirt collar.

Whatever Hazard had been doing, he must have been interrupted when Nico switched off all the fuses.

And now Nico could see what Hazard really was.

He ran towards Hazard and reached for the wire.

Hazard spun towards him and pushed Nico away.

With a furious scream, Ella charged at Hazard and kicked his left knee cap. He winced in pain but shoved her away.

'JUMP HIM!' shouted Nico.

The six of them leaped on him. He fought back with steely resolve, kicking and hitting and chopping, but six against one proved too much, even for him.

When Nico finally managed to reach the panel, he yanked the wire hard. Sparks flew out of Hazard's head.

'STAND BACK!' shouted Ella.

Suddenly bits of Hazard's body started popping out of their joints and he crashed to the ground.

He lay there, a twitching mass of wires, cables and metallic joints. It was a full couple of minutes before his body came to a complete halt.

He lay there on the ground, his glassy eyes showing no pain or emotion.

Whatever he was exactly, he was dead.

CHAPTER 10

'So it wasn't any of us who were the robots,' whispered Jessica, as they all stared at Hazard's lifeless body. 'It was him.'

'What did he mean when he said that thing about studying us for the future of his kind?' said Jules.

'Maybe he wanted to know all about human life, so his robot army could defeat us and take over the Earth,' said Tom.

'Do you think he *has* a robot army?' said Keisha.

'I can't remember any of the last fifteen years,' said Nico, 'so I have no idea about the next ten seconds, let alone years.'

'Well, at least none of *us* are in his robot army, if it exists,' said Jules.

'Let's get out of here,' said Jessica.

They left Hazard lying where he was and explored the building fully.

There were science labs, research stations and tons of equipment. Hazard had an office on the top floor. They pored over documents and computer files.

'Hey, check this out,' said Keisha, thumbing through a green file. 'He didn't lie about finding each of us a family. We all have somewhere to go.'

The others gathered round her and checked out the file. It was all there: the names of the family, their addresses, their correspondence concerning possible adoption of the teenagers.

'So maybe Hazard wasn't all bad,' murmured Ella.

'I think his use of that fire set-up and that room of death is proof that he was all bad,' said Nico.

'You're probably right,' nodded Ella.

Jules printed out all of the necessary information about each of the six's new 'family.' All of the families lived nearby.

Ella then found maps of the local area and printed out six, each one marked with the destination of the teenager's new 'family'.

*****

Half an hour later, using keys they'd found in Hazard's office, they opened a meshed steel gate that led through the barbed wire and they walked out onto a wide and empty country lane.

Together they walked the half-mile or so to a crossroads that was marked on their maps.

There were four turn-offs. Keisha and Jules were going in the same direction, so were Tom and Jessica. Ella was going off by herself, as was Nico.

There were hugs all round and promises that they'd stay in close touch and would report to the others anything they discovered about their previous lives or about Hazard's experiments.

Keisha and Jules headed off, and a short while later Tom and Jessica made tracks. That left Nico and Ella standing at the crossroads.

'I guess this is it, then,' said Nico.

'I guess you're right,' nodded Ella, 'but our families live pretty close to each other, so I'm sure we'll stay in touch.'

Nico grinned and they began walking down their separate roads.

Nico hadn't got far when he heard a cry of pain. He turned round and saw that Ella had tripped and fallen. She had grazed her knee quite badly.

Nico was about to run back and see if she was OK, but Ella called out that she was fine.

As he gave her a parting wave, something caught Nico's eye.

It was only for a split-second, but he was sure that, underneath the grazed skin on Ella's knee, he saw a patch of shimmering, silver metal.

MORE GREAT TOXIC READS

Action-packed adventure stories featuring jungles, swamps, deserted islands, robots, space travel, zombies, computer viruses and monsters from the deep.

How many have you read?

BY ROYAL ORDER OR DEATH

by Jonny Zucker

Miles is a member of the Royal Protection Hub, whose job is to protect the Royal family. When Princess Helena is kidnapped, Miles uncovers a cunning and dangerous plot. Miles must use all his skills to outwit the kidnappers and save the princess's life.

MORE GREAT
TOXIC READS

ZOMBIE CAMP

by Jonny Zucker

Arjun and Kev are at summer camp. It's great – there's lots to do and places to explore. But after a while Arjun and Kev begin to suspect that nothing is quite as it seems. Can they avoid the terrible fate that awaits them?

VIRUS 21

by Jonny Zucker

A new computer virus is rapidly spreading throughout the world. It is infecting everything, closing down hospitals, airports and even the internet. Can Troy and Macy find the hackers before the whole world shuts down?

Jonny Zucker has been a teacher, musician, stand-up comedian and footballer, but now he is best known as one of the most popular authors for children. So far he has written over 100 books.

Jonny also plays in a band and has done over 60 gigs as a stand-up comedian, reaching the London Region Final of the BBC New Comedy awards.

He still dreams of being a professional footballer.